First published in Belgium and Holland by Clavis Uitgeverij, Hasselt – Amsterdam, 2017

English translation from the Dutch by Clavis Publishing Inc. New York

Visit us on the Web at www.clavisbooks.com.

A Book for Benny written by Judith Koppens and illustrated by Marja Meijer
Original title: *Sam en Bennie op zoek naar een boek*
Translated from the Dutch by Clavis Publishing

ISBN 978-1-60537-352-2 (hardback edition)
ISBN 978-1-60537-393-5 (paperback edition)

This book was printed in July 2017 at Publikum d.o.o., Slavka Rodica 6, Belgrade, Serbia.

First Edition
10 9 8 7 6 5 4 3 2 1

Clavis Publishing supports the First Amendment and celebrates the right to read

Judith Koppens & Marja Meijer

A Book for Benny

NEW YORK

It’s raining outside. But that’s okay, because
Sam is warm and cozy inside,
reading a book. Her little dog, Benny,
is not reading. He is tugging on Sam’s sleeve.
“No, Benny,” says Sam.

“I’m not going to play with you.
I’m reading.”

juf

"Reading is fun, you know!" Sam holds her book up to Benny's nose, but Benny walks away. "Maybe you'd like reading too but would prefer a different book?" asks Sam. "That's okay, because there are a lot of fun books."

"Come, Benny. We'll go to the library. We'll pick out a nice book just for you!" Sam puts on her raincoat and Benny cheerfully wags his tail.

He really wants to go outside with Sam.

"Here we are!" Sam cries happily.

They are standing in front of a big building.

Sam and Benny go through the library door. It feels good to be out of the rain.

"I'm sorry, young lady, but dogs are not allowed in here!"
calls a woman behind the counter.
"But Benny wants a book," Sam says proudly. "Just for him!"
"A book for a dog? That's a fun idea," the woman says.
"But I can't let you bring Benny in the library."

"Well, I guess you have to wait outside," says Sam
while she strokes Benny's head. Sam ties Benny to a bike rack.

"You wait here. I'll go and find you a nice book.
I'll be back soon."

“Let’s see,” Sam thinks out loud while she runs her fingers along the spines of the books.

“Yes, a book about knights! That’s perfect for Benny. Benny likes adventure.” She quickly runs to the window with the knight book. She puts the book against the window so Benny can see it. Benny looks up at Sam, but then he pees against the tree.

BOOKS

“Okay, so no book about knights.” Sam runs back to the bookshelves.

“Hmm, let’s see.”

“Yes, a book about the circus! That’s fun for Benny.

Benny loves to do tricks with the ball.”

Sam runs back to the window,
where Benny is still waiting.

"Look, Benny! A book about the circus!"

she calls through the glass.

Benny turns around for a second but then

he turns his back to the window again.

"Okay, okay, so not the circus. But what, then?"

Sam takes a few more books from a box. Princesses, pilots, school…

“Yes, this is the one!” Sam suddenly cries.

She pulls a book from the box and looks for the best picture to show Benny.
Benny looks at the book and starts to wag his tail.

He barks and licks the window... again and again.

The window is dirty, but Benny is happy.

And so is Sam.

She runs to the counter to borrow the book. "Ma'am, I found a perfect book for Benny," she says cheerfully. She hands the book to the woman, who reads the title out loud:

"I Love Sausages: 101 Recipes."

"But that's a cookbook," the library woman says.

"That doesn't matter," says Sam, and she shrugs.

"Benny likes this book best."

Proudly, Sam walks outside to where
Benny is waiting for her. And for his new book.

As soon as they're home, Sam picks up her book
and starts reading again.

And Benny?
He has lovely dreams about his book.

I
sausage